To Christian

2.12.20

WIGGINS PRESS
Published by Wiggins Press
15945 Preswick Lane
Granger, IN 46530
www.wigginspress.com

Copyright © 2015 James Zwerneman

All rights reserved, which includes the right to reproduce this book or portions thereof in any form whatsoever.
For permission requests, contact the publisher at the website above.

The text of this book is set in Minion Pro.
The illustrations are watercolor and ink, reproduced in full color.

Library of Congress control number: 2015912196
ISBN: 978-0-9966331-0-9

Printed in the United States of America
First printing, 2015
10 9 8 7 6 5 4 3 2 1

THE ADVENTURES OF TA AND BODDINGTON

BOOK 1
INTO THE UNKNOWN

BY
JAMES ZWERNEMAN

WP

Wiggins Press

Once upon a time
there was a caveman named Ta.
He lived in a hole under a hill
in the Great Green Forest.

A long time ago
he had chased out the bears
living in the cave.

Now the cave was home.
It was safe and warm and dry.
Ta set it up just how he liked it.

The forest was wonderful.
There were trees for climbing,
rivers for fishing and swimming in,
and turkeys for hunting.

Most of all,
there were blueberries for eating.
Ta liked to drizzle honey on his blueberries.

Ta had everything he needed to survive,
but he was lonely.
He often wondered if there were others
living in the Unknown.

One day he decided to see.
He gathered all the supplies he would need.
One drum. One bag of water.
One pouch of blueberries drizzled in honey
to share with his new friend.

Then he gathered his courage and set out.

He searched high.

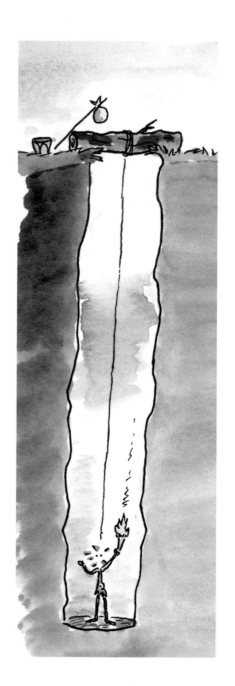

He searched low.

But he couldn't find a friend anywhere.
He began to wonder if he should have stayed at home.

One night it got so cold
Ta could hardly move his frozen hands to drum.
Still, he kept at it.
He was about to fall asleep, when…

It was a caveman!

"Hello, I'm Boddington," said the caveman. "Pleased to meet you."

Was this a friend at last?

Boddington was very hungry.
He ate the rest of the blueberries.

They began home at once.
Ta was excited to show his new friend
all the neat things in the Great Green Forest.

Suddenly they heard something coming.

"It's them!" said Boddington.

SWISH!
SWISH!

They ran and ran.
But the noise came closer.

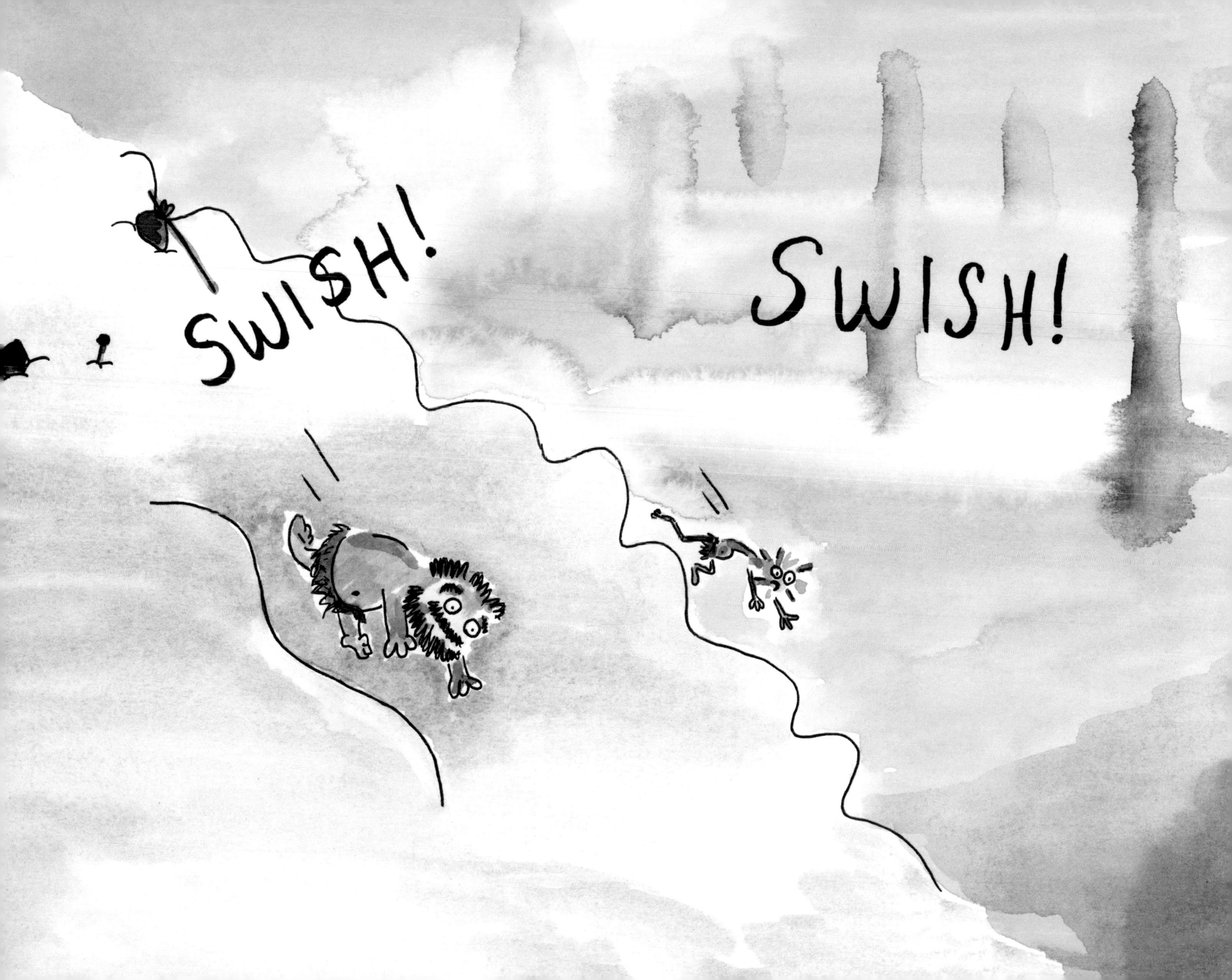
SWISH!
SWISH!

It was a cavewoman!

"Hi, I'm Sally," she said.
"You forgot your drum."

Sally was an inventor.
She had invented skis!
If you ever go skiing someday,
remember to thank Sally.

She made two new pairs.
One for Boddington.
One for Ta.

Ta was delighted with his new skis,
but he was even happier to have made another friend.
Two friends in one morning:
this was the best day of his life!

Sally and Boddington loved the Great Green Forest, especially the blueberries drizzled in honey.

They loved the cave, too.
"You're very talented, Ta," said Sally.
Ta was pleased.
Boddington liked the drums.

But they were not alone.
"It's them!" said Boddington.

Before, there had been too much space.
Now, there was not enough!

"This is nice," said the cave people.
"Hooray for Ta!"

Luckily, Sally was an inventor.
She had an idea…

Little caves – for everyone!
Sally named them "houses."
This is why we live in houses today.

"Thank you, Sally," said Ta.

With Sally's help,
Ta even built a place for the bears to stay.

Everyone was very happy,
and Ta did not feel lonely anymore.

The End

Books in the Ta and Boddington series

Book 1 - Into the Unknown
Book 2 - The Chief's Dilemma
Book 3 - Boddington and the Bicycle
Book 4 - An Unexpected Visitor

Available from Wiggins Press
www.wigginspress.com